HEAD OVER HEELS

Adapted by Paul Mantell
Based on the series created by Gordon Korman

New York

CONTENTS

THE JERSEY

HEAD OVER HEELS

CHAPTER ONE

SKATEBOARD MANIAC!

Elliott Rifkin pushed off with his back foot and guided his skateboard down the street that skirted the park grounds. He crouched down, lowering his center of gravity and gaining speed rapidly. It was show time!

Leaning back and hitting the kickplate with his right foot, he hopped over the low curb and onto the sidewalk. Then he popped a wheelie and rolled down the sidewalk on his rear wheels.

Elliott stamped down on the kickplate again and leaped into the air, his board floating up onto one of the bus stop benches that lined the sidewalk. Elliott rode the board along the seat of the bench, and then hopped down again, still rolling.

He could hear his Monday Night Football Club buddies cheering him on as they watched from a distance. But Elliott was too busy concentrating on his next move to acknowledge them. He knew that if he wanted to be a champion skateboarder, like his idol Tony Hawk, he had to maintain his focus at all times.

As Elliott turned around and headed back toward his pals, he launched into a series of step turns. He "walked the board around" by kicking down on the front and bringing the back end around and forward, all the while spinning his body in a circle to keep the rotation going.

Then he flipped his board, kicking it up with his back foot and turning it over with his front foot, until it was right side up again!

For his grand finale, Elliott hopped the bench again, this time with an incredible vertical leap, sending his board as high as the back of the bench before coming safely down on its surface. He dropped back down onto the sidewalk and skidded to a stop with his fists raised high in victory.

"You're the skateboard master, Elliott!" shouted his friend Nick Lighter, unofficial leader of the Monday Night Football Club. Nick, Elliott, and their friends, Morgan and Coleman, were all sports fanatics: that's why they had formed the club in the first place. But none of the others could even come close to Elliott's prowess on a skateboard.

Nick had founded the club, and he was also the owner of the magic jersey. He'd inherited it from his grandfather, and it was the coolest thing Elliott had ever seen or experienced. It seemed crazy, but the jersey had the ability to transport an ordinary kid into the body of a real, live, professional sports star! Elliott hadn't believed it at first. But then the jersey had transported Nick right into an NFL game—as San Francisco 49er, Steve Young. And another time, it had "jumped" Nick and Morgan into a major-league baseball game. Needless to say, the MNFC members were in complete awe of the jersey's ability to make their wildest sports dreams come true.

Nick guarded the magic jersey like the

treasure it was, and it cemented his role as the MNFC's fearless leader.

"Whoo-oo!" Nick's cousin Morgan shouted, clapping her hands. "That was amazing, Elliott! Fantastic!"

Morgan was the newest member of the club. A few months before, she had moved to town from Chicago with her mom. Morgan could keep up with any of her male buddies in almost every sport. And in some, like basketball, she was better than all of them. She also had an amazing encyclopedic knowledge of sports statistics and trivia. As far as Elliott was concerned, Morgan was really cool.

Coleman was applauding, too, as he sat perched on his bike. He gave Elliott a thumbs-up, and followed it up with a MNFC handshake, complete with their patented finger snap. Coleman, or "'Slaw," was Elliott's best friend. They'd known each other since they were in diapers, but they had promised each other that they'd never show those embarrassing baby pictures to anyone else.

'Slaw was about a foot taller than Elliott, and built like a linebacker. But other than that, the two boys were a lot alike. They were both A+ students, and they were into all the same things—except that 'Slaw preferred trick biking to skateboarding. His idol was Dave Mirra, "The Miracle Man."

"Good show, E-man!" Coleman said.

"Thanks!" Elliott replied, flush with triumph. He was sure that this had been his best routine ever. If he kept at it for a couple more years, maybe he could be performing exhibitions on TV, just like Tony Hawk.

Coleman checked his watch. "Uh-oh. Catch you later, guys," he said, and pedaled off down the street on his bike.

"'Catch you later?'" Nick repeated in disbelief. "Where are you going? The Cowboys and Jets kick off at seven o'clock!"

It was Monday afternoon, which meant that there would be an official meeting of the Monday Night Football Club that evening. Every week, they gathered in the Lighters' den to watch the game on Nick's big-screen TV. As far as Elliott was concerned, it was the most fun a sports fan could possibly have—unless you were actually *in* the game.

"Uh . . . I—I—I . . . I've just got a . . . a thing to do, that's all," Coleman said, not looking back as he rode away. "Catch you later!"

They all watched him go. "A 'thing'? What's a 'thing'?" Morgan wondered out loud, a puzzled expression on her face.

Elliott had a snappy answer at the ready. "A thing is an entity, idea, or quality, thought to have its own existence. Try reading the dictionary, my friend," Elliott advised, clapping Morgan on the back affectionately. "Hey, check out this new trick. I'm thinking of sending it to Tony Hawk!"

Tightening the chinstrap on his helmet, Elliott pushed off. His face was set in deep concentration. He sped straight for the park bench. Then, an instant before he would have crashed into it, he jumped up, leaving his board on the ground. The board rolled under the bench while Elliott ran across the seat of the bench. He dropped right back onto the board on the other side.

Elliott expected to hear another round of cheers from Nick and Morgan. Instead, they were calling his name urgently. Elliott turned to look at them—big mistake!—only to see Nick pointing earnestly at something in Elliott's path.

"Look out!" Morgan shouted. "Elliott! Oh, no!!"

Elliott turned to look ahead of him again, and saw what they were warning him about. A man in a baseball cap was getting out of his car, carrying two grocery bags full of food—and he was about to back right into Elliott.

"Aaaahhhh!" Elliott screamed. There was no time to steer clear. He slammed right into the man, sending him sprawling backward onto the sidewalk. The bags of food went flying in every direction. Out of one of them came a big, gooey chocolate cake. It flew into the air, turning over and over. Elliott watched as it came down—as if in slow motion—and landed right in the man's face.

Elliott had somehow managed to stay on his board. Now, he stepped off and grabbed it, then ran back to help. "Sorry! I'm really sorry!" he cried, bending down over the man and helping to remove the cake from his face. Morgan and Nick ran over, too, crouching down to pick up the stray groceries and put them back in the bags.

The man stared up at Elliott, stunned, blinking at him through a face full of chocolate. "Mphmrgrnh," he moaned, his mouth still stuffed full of cake.

Suddenly, a long shadow loomed over them all. Elliott looked up, and found himself staring into the face of a huge, hulking policeman.

"It . . . it was an accident!" Elliott tried to explain.

The policeman's face was expressionless. Without a word, he pointed with his nightstick to a sign posted on a nearby tree. The sign, in big white letters, read: No Skateboarding or Rollerblading on Park Property.

Elliott swallowed hard. "I . . . I . . . uh . . . I'm *really* sorry!"

The policeman put out an empty hand, palm upward, and pointed with his nightstick to Elliott's skateboard. "Let's have it, son," he ordered.

Elliott handed over the board, a sinking feeling in his stomach. He wished a hole would open in the ground, so he could jump into it and disappear.

CHAPTER TWO

A BLOW FOR PERSONAL FREEDOM

"I can't believe this!" Elliott moaned. He paced back and forth in the Lighters' kitchen while Morgan and Nick fixed snacks. It was seven o'clock, and the game would be starting any minute.

But Elliott wasn't through complaining. "It was an accident!" he protested, as if the policeman were still there. "I can't believe he took it from me!"

"Take it easy, Elliott," Nick said.

"I've *got* to board," Elliott insisted. "I *live* to board!" He banged his fist down on the countertop. "Held down by 'the man' again!"

Morgan rolled her eyes. "You're getting your board back in a month," she reminded him. "Relax!"

"Oh, yeah?" Elliott countered. "*You* try losing *your* identity for a month, and see how you like it."

The more Elliott thought about it, the angrier he got. Was it his fault if there was no good place to board in this stupid town? He'd been exercising his constitutional right to freedom of expression, and the long arm of the law had reached out to stop him! It was not only unfair; it was downright unconstitutional!

"They may have taken my board," Elliott shouted, "but they can't take away my freedom!"

Morgan shook her head, smiling, and sighed. Nick carried the bowls of snack food into the den, then came back into the kitchen, carrying a football.

"Hey, where's Coleman?" he asked. "He's never been late for Monday Night Football." He passed the ball to Morgan, who caught it with one hand, without even looking.

"He didn't even call?" Morgan asked.

Nick picked up the kitchen phone, and dialed Coleman's number. But there was no answer, because at that moment, Coleman came through the Lighters' front door and waltzed into the kitchen.

Morgan heaved a huge sigh of relief, mingled with annoyance. "Hey, 'Slaw, where have you been?" she asked.

"Yeah," said Nick. "The game's already started." Inside the den, they could hear the roar of the crowd on TV as the Jets kicked off against the Cowboys.

Coleman took a step back. "Whoa," he said. "What's the big deal? I just had some homework to do."

Nick eyed him suspiciously. "'Slaw, it takes you five minutes to do your homework," he pointed out.

"Hey, I'm here now," 'Slaw said, sounding annoyed. "So let's just watch the game, okay?"

Now it was the others' turn to back off. "Okay," Nick muttered.

"Okay," Morgan echoed softly.

"That's what I'm talking about," Coleman muttered, brushing past them and heading for the den. "Come on. Let's watch some Monday Night Football."

At halftime, they went back out into the kitchen to refill the snack bowls and put more ice in their glasses. Nick, Morgan, and 'Slaw were all talking excitedly about the game.

But Elliott had barely been able to focus on football. He had no idea what the score was, and he didn't care. His mind was still on what had happened that afternoon. He couldn't get that policeman's angry glare out of his head.

What a travesty! The blatant injustice of it all! What did this town have against skateboarders anyway? Where were they supposed to express their artistry, if not at the park?

"I know!" he said out loud, snapping his fingers as the brilliant flash of an idea came to him. "We'll build our own half-pipe!" He clapped his hands in self-congratulation. "Yes! This is genius! No one can hold down a Rifkin!" He leaped into the air, his fists raised in triumph.

After a few seconds, he realized that his friends weren't jumping around the room with him. In fact, they seemed completely unimpressed with his stroke of genius.

"Elliott," Morgan said, giving him a dubious look, "how are you going to build a half-pipe? I mean, where would you put it?"

Elliott sighed patiently. "Do you think they asked Donald Trump where he'd put the Trump Tower?" he asked.

Morgan put her hands on her hips. "Uh . . . *yeah*," she said.

Elliott scowled. "Bad example," he admitted, trying to think of another way to get his point across.

Just then, Nick's dad, Mr. Lighter, came in from outside. "Hey, guys!" he greeted them. Mr. Lighter had an ice cream cone in his hand, and was licking it contentedly.

"All I need is someone's backyard," Elliott continued, still stuck on his half-pipe idea.

"Don't look at me," Morgan said, shrugging. "I live in an apartment, re-member?"

"Coleman?" Elliott asked, giving his friend a pleading look.

Coleman shook his head sadly. "No one goes near our yard without a professional degree in horticulture," he reminded Elliott. 'Slaw's mom took a lot of pride in her garden. The MNFC wasn't even allowed to play *football* in Coleman's yard!

"I need my half-pipe!" Elliott insisted.

Nick, Morgan, and Coleman headed

back to the den, as Mr. Lighter came up to Elliott.

"Elliott, I heard you had a little run-in with the law," he said in a hushed tone.

"Uh, yeah," Elliott said, feeling himself blushing. "I think constitutional issues are involved."

"I agree," Mr. Lighter said seriously, to Elliott's surprise. "You know, I couldn't help overhear you talking about a half-pipe. And, well, I've got a lot of room in the lot down at my store. . . ."

"Really?" Elliott asked hopefully. Mr. Lighter owned a sporting goods store, and the place did have a really big parking lot. "Can we build it there?"

"Sure!" Mr. Lighter said. "I'll even help! It'll be fun." He threw an arm around Elliott's shoulders. "We'll show 'em!"

"All right!" Elliott said excitedly. "Us

against 'the system,' Mr. Lighter. A blow for personal freedom!"

Mr. Lighter flashed a peace sign. "Feels like the '60s all over again," he said with a mischievous grin.

CHAPTER THREE

IF YOU BUILD IT, THEY WILL COME

Nick came up to Morgan at her locker after lunch on Thursday. "Have you noticed something?" he asked.

"What's to notice?" Morgan replied.

Nick frowned. How could Morgan be so oblivious? "We haven't seen 'Slaw in three days, duh," he said.

Morgan shrugged. "He's probably just doing other stuff."

"Like what?" Nick challenged her.

Morgan thought it over for a minute. "You're right," she said. "'Slaw never has anything better to do than hang with us."

"I think we should go find him," Nick suggested. "We've got five minutes till next period."

"Good idea." They marched over to Coleman's locker and found him there, unloading books from his backpack.

"Hey, 'Slaw, where have you been?" Morgan said, jumping right in.

"We didn't see you at lunch all week," added Nick. "What's up?"

Coleman frowned, and looked down at his shoes. "I had things to do," he mumbled.

"'Things?'" Nick mimicked him. "Things like what?"

Coleman shut his locker and wheeled around to face Nick. "What are you, my mother?" he asked, agitated.

Morgan jumped in between them to keep the peace. "Guys, just chill, okay?" Then she turned to Coleman. "You coming next Monday night, 'Slaw?"

Coleman smiled at her, nodding. "I'll be there," he assured her. "Wouldn't miss it." Then he looked at Nick, scowling. "I've gotta get to my Latin class." Shouldering his book bag, he sauntered off down the hall.

Nick shook his head. "Something's up with him," he said.

All week long at school, Elliott thought about the half-pipe. It was going to be so awesome to have a place to practice his stunts without getting in trouble.

But Elliott wasn't planning to hog the half-pipe all to himself. He'd invite 'Slaw to use it, so that "the next Dave Mirra" could get better at his bicycle stunts. And all the other skateboarders and trick bikers in town could come and use it, too, Elliott decided, feeling distinctly generous.

Soon, there it would be, in all its glory: the centerpiece of the store's parking lot, and a beacon of freedom to all the sports rebels in town! "Yeah," shouted Elliott.

"Excuse me, Mr. Rifkin? Did you have something you wanted to tell the class?"

Elliott snapped out of his daydream and blinked back at Mr. Chambers, his history teacher. Oops. Had he really shouted out loud in the middle of class? "Uh, no, Mr. Chambers," he said sheepishly. "Thanks, anyway." The whole class erupted in laughter, and Elliott sank as low as he could in his chair.

But Saturday morning finally came, and all the daydreaming and the frustration of waiting were over. As he walked to the store parking lot, he was actually humming to himself. Elliott figured they'd finish the half-pipe in a few hours. The hardest thing after that would be waiting the three weeks to get his skateboard back so he could use it.

There was Nick's dad now, waving to him. Mr. Lighter was wearing his work belt, with all kinds of neat tools hanging from it. Elliott didn't know what any of them were called, except for the hammer and screwdrivers. But that didn't matter. He was sure that building the half-pipe was going to be a breeze. How could it not be? After all, it was just a big curvy ramp made out of wood.

Mr. Lighter was bent over a roll of blueprints, laid out on a piece of plywood supported by two sawhorses. Nearby was a workbench with power tools on it, and a truck piled high with lumber.

"Wow!" Elliott exclaimed. Mr. Lighter was really going all out.

"Hi!" he said to Elliott, then handed him a pair of safety goggles, a tool belt, and a yellow hard hat. "Here. Put these on," he said. "Safety first!"

Mr. Lighter seemed even more cheerful than usual. He kept humming a tune that Elliott knew was from the '60s, though he didn't know the name of it. Elliott put on his belt and goggles, then strapped on the hat. "Whoa, this is so cool!" he said, checking himself out in the reflection of the store's window.

He went over to where Mr. Lighter was standing, and looked over his shoulder at the big roll of blueprints. "Awesome!" Elliott exclaimed.

Mr. Lighter shrugged. "Well, the drawings were on the Internet, so I figured, why not go for it?" He looked around. "Where are the other kids?"

Elliott sighed. He hated to break the news to Mr. Lighter. He knew Nick's dad had been counting on a bigger workforce than just the two of them.

"They don't share our vision, Mr. Lighter," Elliott said, putting a consoling hand on his shoulder. "Plus, they had homework."

He didn't mention that Coleman had totally avoided him; doing "things" he wouldn't tell Elliott about. He was starting to get worried about 'Slaw, who normally would have been there helping, for sure. Yes, something was definitely up with him. . . .

"So, I guess it's just you and me," Mr.

Lighter said. "Well, my man . . . are you handy?"

"Um . . . sure!" Elliott said, giving him a big smile.

"Good! Then let's get to work."

Elliott followed Mr. Lighter to the truck, and they started unloading different lengths of lumber. Boy, wood sure is heavy, Elliott reflected, huffing and puffing to hold up his end of the stack of boards.

Next, Elliott handed the boards to Mr. Lighter one by one, so he could saw them into the proper lengths. Then it was time to put all the pieces together. Elliott took out his hammer, and started pounding nails. He swung it way over his head on each stroke, to make sure he was getting maximum power.

"Uh, not like that, Elliott," Mr. Lighter

said, wincing. He came over and showed Elliott how to take a shorter stroke, so that the hammer actually hit the nail.

After about an hour, Elliott was feeling totally exhausted. He sat down to rest while Mr. Lighter kept on hammering away.

Boy, thought Elliott, this was taking way longer than he'd thought it would. So far, they'd only built a couple of pieces of framing! The way Elliott had imagined it, the half-pipe should have been half done by now. But he could see that they weren't going to finish it today—or even *next* Saturday. He wondered if his half-pipe would even be ready by the time he got his skateboard back.

Elliott opened his eyes. He must have fallen asleep, sitting there on the asphalt. There were more framed sections now, lying on the pavement. He wondered how long

Mr. Lighter had been working without him.

"Okay, Mr. Lighter," Elliott said, dusting himself off. A cloud of sawdust hung in the air around him. "Ready to put these together?"

Mr. Lighter turned and saw Elliott sitting there. "Oh. Taking a break, huh? Well, that's okay. You've been working hard for . . ." He checked his watch. "Wow . . . three hours gone already!" He looked at the frames on the ground. "Not bad for just the two of us," he said.

Elliott bit his lip. He didn't want to tell Mr. Lighter it had been just the *one* of him for the last two hours. He hadn't even noticed Elliott napping!

"Now," Mr. Lighter said, "crouch down here and hold this piece while I nail it onto the side."

Elliott did as he was told, and Mr.

Lighter proceeded to nail crossbeams onto the section of half-pipe. When he was done, Mr. Lighter walked away—with Elliott trapped inside the finished section!

"Um, Mr. Lighter?" Elliott called after him. "Larry? Please . . . I'm stuck in here!"

An hour later, one end of the half-pipe was finally in place. Curved pieces of particleboard were nailed to the sides. All that was missing were the thin plywood layers that would make up the skating surface.

"Lookin' good," Elliott said, surveying their day's handiwork. He clapped his partner on the back, sending another cloud of sawdust into the air. "Larry, my man, I couldn't have done it without you!"

CHAPTER FOUR

'SLAW'S SURPRISE

It was seven o'clock on Monday night—time for the Steelers-Dolphins game to begin. In the Lighters' den, Nick had the football in his hands and was trying to pass it over the couch to Morgan. Elliott stood in front of her, trying to intercept the pass. But all the while, Elliott was yammering on about his half-pipe, and Nick was starting to get tired of it. He and Morgan had already gotten an earful at school that day.

"Yesss!" Elliott was saying now. "It is happening! Our own half-pipe! No 'policia' to tell us 'No skateboarding. City ordinance.'"

Nick threw the football right over Elliott's upraised hands to the taller Morgan, who reached up high to grab it.

Elliott made only a halfhearted effort to bat the ball away. Then, a puzzled look came over his face. "Hey," he said. "Where's Coleman?"

"Again? This is getting ridiculous," Morgan commented, tossing the football back to Nick.

"Okay, Elliott," said Nick. "You be center and hike it to me on three," Nick said. Morgan lined up on Nick's left, all three of them with their backs to the door.

But before they could begin the play, they heard footsteps coming down the hall. "Hey, guys!" said Coleman, entering the den.

Nick got up and turned around. "Coleman, where have you—"

He fell suddenly silent, staring in dumbfounded amazement. Coleman was there, all right, but he was not alone. Smiling at Nick over 'Slaw's left shoulder was—a girl! A really, really *pretty* girl, Nick noticed. She had one hand on Coleman's shoulder, and she was smiling at them all with a perfect, white, gorgeous set of teeth.

"Guys," Coleman said proudly, beaming at the girl. "This is Hannah. Hannah, *this* is the MNFC."

Nick tore his gaze away from Hannah and looked over at the others to see how they were reacting.

Elliott's face was frozen in an open-mouthed stare, just the way Nick imagined he himself looked. Morgan was blinking rapidly, but at least she managed to say something.

"Another girl for a change!" she welcomed Hannah with a warm smile. "Welcome to the Monday Night Football Club. That's what we call ourselves."

Hannah raised one eyebrow in a look of amused surprise. "A club?" she said. "Cute."

Nick caught the look she was giving them—as if they were a bunch of overgrown toddlers. "'Slaw," he said, arching an eyebrow, "you kind of took us by surprise."

"Yeah, I know," Coleman said, laughing, as if it were just fine and dandy that he'd brought a guest into the inner sanctum of the very exclusive MNFC.

"'Slaw?' That's what they call you?" Hannah said. "That's your nickname? How precious." Coleman grinned bashfully and looked away, digging his toe into the carpet.

An uncomfortable silence descended on the room. Once again, Morgan came to the rescue. "So . . ." she said, "why don't you guys have a seat?" She indicated one of the two couches, each big enough for two people to sit comfortably.

'Slaw led Hannah over to the right-hand couch, while Elliott, football in hand, leaped onto the other one. Nick plopped down next to him, in his usual position.

"Hey," Elliott said to Nick, in a voice loud enough for Hannah and Coleman to overhear, "isn't bringing a stranger illegal?"

Nick noticed Hannah and Coleman exchanging wary glances before sitting down.

Morgan said, "Scoot over, Nick." She sat down on his right, forcing him to move over. "Keep going," she said, edging him more and more to the left, until Elliott was crowded right off the end of the couch. "Okay, good," Morgan said, settling in to watch the game.

Elliott, having lost their little game of musical chairs, was the odd man out. "Hey!" he complained. "We have a seating arrangement here! Why do I have to move because Coleman brought a guest—*unannounced*?"

"Elliott, don't be a whiner—just sit on the floor," Morgan told him.

But Elliott, in "rebel mode" all week long, was in no mood to back down, even if the person he was confronting was his best friend, 'Slaw. "Nine years of my life I dedicate to you guys, and I have to sit on the floor? No!" he said, sitting down right on the coffee table.

Nick found himself staring at Elliott's back instead of the football game. "Elliott, move!" he demanded. "I can't see."

Elliott slid over to the other side of the coffee table.

"Hey!" Morgan cried. "Now *I* can't see!"

Elliott, uttering a long sigh of frustration, and giving Nick and Morgan a dirty look, sank onto the floor.

Nick felt sorry for him. Elliott had a point, after all. 'Slaw had no right to bring a stranger here without asking them. Not even a beautiful stranger like Hannah. "You know, 'Slaw, Elliott's right," he said. "We do have rules for the MNFC."

"Yeah," Morgan agreed. "Like I had to take that entrance exam," she reminded Nick.

Nick would rather have forgotten. When Morgan had first come to town, Nick hadn't wanted any girls in the MNFC. Even though she was a true jock and a storehouse of sports stats, he'd found Morgan's presence threatening. So Nick had devised an impossible test for her to pass in order to be admitted to the club. Of course, Morgan had passed with flying colors, humiliating Nick. He had *had* to let her in.

Now, of course, he was glad he had. Morgan was one of the guys as far as he was concerned, even though she was definitely a girl. But letting in more outsiders was another thing.

"Hey, I know football," Hannah said,

sitting up on the sofa. "Come on. Give me a test!"

Elliott sighed in exasperation. "Can we please just watch the game?" he moaned.

They all turned their attention to the screen. The Dolphins' quarterback dropped back to pass and threw the ball into the end zone for a touchdown.

"What a play!" Nick exclaimed excitedly.

"Touchdown!" the announcer yelled. Then, "Uh-oh, there's a flag on the play."

"Offside. Right tackle flinched," Hannah said quickly, pointing at the screen.

"No way!" Nick said. "I didn't see anything."

The announcer's voice continued, "You really had to be watching to catch that one. The Dolphins' right tackle barely moved, but it was a tough call. So the Steelers catch a huge break here. . . ."

Nick blinked in astonishment. Hannah had called it perfectly, when even he himself hadn't noticed anything! He looked over at Hannah, who was wearing a smug smile. She settled back into Coleman's arms. "I just love the Steelers," she cooed. "Kordell Stewart is sooo cute!"

"Isn't she great?" Coleman said, gazing at Hannah like she was an angel from heaven.

Elliott turned to Hannah, annoyed beyond endurance. "We do have rules, and one of them's about talking during the game," he told her. "It's: DON'T."

Hannah didn't back off an inch. "There are eighty thousand screaming fans," she pointed out, "but *we* have to be quiet?"

"Uh-huh," Nick said, nodding. The

rules were the rules, and Elliott was right. While the game was on, nobody talked. It had always been that way, and it always would be.

"And you come here every Monday?" Hannah asked Coleman, making a face. "That's almost sad."

'Slaw put an arm around her shoulders. Nick, Morgan, and Elliott exchanged worried glances as Coleman whispered in Hannah's ear. The two of them giggled, giving each other sidelong glances. Nick knew the joke had to be at the MNFC's expense.

So *this* was what Coleman had been up to all week!

CHAPTER FIVE

FOOLS RUSH IN

At school the next morning, Nick and Elliott huddled around Elliott's locker. There hadn't been time the night before to talk about Coleman and Hannah, because they'd all been right there together in the room.

"We're his friends," Nick was saying. "And if he likes her, then we should be nice to her."

Elliott gritted his teeth. "But we vote

on new members," he reminded Nick. "And who says we allow 'guests'?" Elliott slammed his locker shut. Why was Nick standing up for this girl, anyway? Was it because she was so pretty?

"Shhh!" Nick warned him. "Here comes 'Slaw. Act normal."

Coleman ambled up to them, smiling like he was on top of the world. "Hey, guys!" he greeted them. "Hey, Elliott, how's that half-pipe coming along?"

"It'll be ready in a couple of weeks— quicker if you come down on Saturday and help out."

"Yeah, well . . . I'm kind of busy these days," Coleman said, smiling and looking down at the floor.

"Anyway, in a couple of weeks, you'll be able to bring your bike down there and practice," Elliott told him. "I've got the plans here in my locker. Wanna take a look?"

"Sure!" Coleman said eagerly.

But just then, Hannah came around the corner of the hallway, and saw them standing there. She gave them a little wave and started in their direction.

"Oh, but look," Elliott said, with a mocking tone in his voice, "Hannah's here."

She came up to Coleman and slipped an arm through his. "'Slaw," she said, a troubled look on her face, "we're sitting with my friends in study hall. Remember?"

"Oh!" Coleman said hurriedly. "Uh, yeah." He smiled sheepishly at her. Turning to Elliott and Nick, he shrugged apologetically. "Hey, I'll . . . I'll catch you guys later," he said, as Hannah led him away.

Elliott watched them go, shaking his head. "Stick a fork in him," he said. "He's done."

Nick sighed wistfully. "I never thought 'Slaw would be the one," he said.

Elliott wrinkled his brow. "What one?" he asked.

"The first one to leave us for a girl," Nick explained.

"I know," Elliott agreed, following Nick's gaze. "I thought it would be me, too."

Nick looked him up and down. "You?"

"Yes, of course," Elliott replied, blinking back at him. "Who else?"

Nick shook his head, smiling. "Never mind."

About a week later, Nick and Morgan were in the school library. They didn't usually hang out there after school, but their English teacher had just assigned them a huge midterm research paper.

"I don't even know who Ernest Hemingway is!" Nick complained. "I'm supposed to do a paper on his life and work?"

"You *chose* Hemingway, remember?" Morgan reminded him. "Mrs. Conboy gave us a whole list of authors."

"Who'd you pick again?"

"Herman Melville." When Nick gave her a blank stare, Morgan rolled her eyes and sighed. "*Moby Dick?* Boy, Nick, do you ever read books?"

"I read sports books," he shot back.

"You read *Sports Illustrated.* That's not a book," Morgan corrected him. "Come on, let's get some research materials."

Just then, they heard Coleman's voice

coming from behind a nearby bookshelf. "No, see, that was back in ancient Babylonia," 'Slaw was saying. "This was during the Roman Empire. Much later."

Morgan put a finger to her lips, motioning for Nick to be quiet. Then she removed a book from the shelf, creating a peephole that she could see through. Nick did the same, and they both leaned in for a closer look.

Coleman was sitting at one of the library tables with Hannah, who had a notebook open in front of her. 'Slaw was thumbing through a fat encyclopedia volume.

Finding the page he wanted, Coleman pointed to it. "Here," he said. "See? This is a portrait of him. Justinian was the emperor. And he created one of the first uniform legal systems."

Biting her lip, Hannah nodded and began to write in her notebook. "First uniform . . ." she mumbled as she wrote. "I'm so slow," she said with a frustrated pout. She moved her face closer to Coleman's. "Could you write that name down for me?" She pushed her notebook toward him.

"Sure," Coleman said, taking the pencil from her and spelling out the name. "There. There you go." He pushed the notebook back toward her.

"And while you're at it," Hannah said, "could you write down a couple of notes about the other stuff he did?" She gazed into his eyes. "My wrist is hurting so bad. . . ."

"I . . . guess I could," Coleman said softly. He began scribbling away, smiling contentedly. "You say you need a three-page paper?" he asked Hannah.

"Uh, yeah," Hannah answered. "But I bet she'd give me extra credit if I handed in five. . . ."

Coleman looked up at her, and Hannah batted her eyelashes at him. Sighing with utter happiness, he went back to writing.

Nick put the book back on the shelf, and looked at Morgan intently. "Boy, I don't know," he whispered, indicating Hannah with a nod of his head. "You're a member of her tribe. What do you think?"

A member of her tribe? thought Morgan. Ugh! Why did Nick have to be such a Neanderthal?

"I say, 'Good for 'Slaw!'" she told Nick with a shrug. "He seems happier than he's ever been. Just an opinion."

Morgan returned to her research while Nick stood there thinking it over for a second. Morgan was right; Coleman did seem as happy as a clam. But something about what he had just seen made Nick wonder if Hannah had 'Slaw's best interests at heart.

CHAPTER SIX

A DIRTY LITTLE SECRET

Two Saturdays after they had begun building it, the half-pipe was finally finished. The red paint Elliott and Mr. Lighter had rolled onto the plywood surface was completely dry. They'd just finished painting the sides blue, and before that, they'd done the decks in yellow.

The half-pipe was a thing of beauty, Elliott told himself contentedly. Too bad he had to wait another whole week before he got his board back!

Mr. Lighter turned to Elliott, holding Nick's skateboard in his hands. "Go for it," he said, holding the board out to him.

It was almost too good to be true! "Are . . . are you sure?" he asked Mr. Lighter.

"Sure, I'm sure, Elliott!" he said. "Gotta test out our handiwork, don't we?"

"Yeah!" Elliott said, taking the board. He grabbed a helmet and strapped it on, bubbling over with excitement. "But what about the police?" he asked.

"They took away your skateboard for a month," Mr. Lighter said with a shrug. "They didn't say you couldn't *borrow* one. Come on, give it a test run!"

Elliott perched himself on the lip of the half-pipe, his right foot on the rear kick-plate of Nick's board. Then he came down with his front foot, launching himself down the ramp. "Elliott Rifkin, droppin' in," he said, playing the announcer as well as the boarder.

"Whoo-oo!" he yelled as he roared across the smooth wooden surface, up the other side, and into the air. Then he spun around and came back down, heading back the other way goofy-style. "Yeah!"

"All right!" Mr. Lighter yelled, applauding. "Lookin' good, my man!"

Elliott went back and forth, performing one turn after the other. Finally, he flipped the board up into the air and caught it as he stepped back onto the lip with Mr. Lighter.

"Pure perfection!" Elliott exulted, patting Mr. Lighter on the shoulder.

Mr. Lighter took the helmet off Elliott's head and put it on his own. It was much too small on him, and looked kind of ridiculous, Elliott thought. But Mr.

Lighter didn't seem to care.

"You know," he told Elliott, "I used to skateboard a bit. May I?"

"Is that a good idea?" Elliott asked warily. "I mean, they didn't have half-pipes back in your day . . . and this one's kind of steep."

"Ahh, come on," Mr. Lighter said, brushing off the warning. "Give me the board."

Elliott handed it over, and Mr. Lighter put his back foot down on it. Letting out a rebel yell, he launched himself down the ramp.

Immediately, Elliott knew Mr. Lighter was in trouble. Maybe it was the flailing arms, or the wobbling knees, or the yell that turned into a scream as he went tumbling and the skateboard went flying into the air.

"Owww!" Mr. Lighter groaned loudly. "Ooowwwww!!"

Elliott winced. This did not look good.

For the past three weeks, Morgan had been doing her best to be nice to Hannah. She waved to her whenever she saw her around school. She talked to her in the cafeteria line. And most of all, she made sure neither Nick nor Elliott were mean to Hannah when she came over with 'Slaw to watch the Monday Night Football games.

Nick and Elliott were just jealous, Morgan realized. The fact that their buddy 'Slaw had a girlfriend before they did was making them both green with envy. Morgan chuckled at the thought of it. Boys could be so ridiculous!

On the other hand, she thought, Hannah wasn't exactly the warmest person—except, of course, with 'Slaw. In fact, she'd been downright cold to the rest of them—even to Morgan—always acting too busy to talk.

It was Monday once again, and that evening they would have another MNFC get-together. As Morgan took some books from her locker, she wondered if 'Slaw would show up, what with Elliott and Nick being so hostile to his girlfriend. Morgan hoped that he would. Monday nights hadn't been the same lately, but they'd be no fun at all if Coleman stopped coming altogether!

Here came Hannah now, walking down the hall with her friend, Kim. Morgan ran to catch up with them. "Hannah!" she called out. "Hey! How's it going?"

"Perfect!" Hannah said, giving Morgan a smile.

There, thought Morgan, comforting herself. She's not so bad after all.

"So . . ." Morgan continued, making conversation. "You and Coleman seem to be hanging out a lot."

"Yeah, he's great," Hannah acknowledged. "And he's so smart!"

"Please!" Kim broke in. "He's amazing. He totally does all her homework. He even wrote—"

Hannah quickly cut her off. "Coleman just . . . helps me," she explained, giving Kim a killer sidelong glance when she thought Morgan wasn't looking.

"Well, *someone* has to help you," Kim shot right back. Turning to Morgan, she explained, "Hannah got put on scholastic probation."

Hannah looked as if she'd just been kicked in the gut. Morgan knew how she felt, because she was feeling exactly the same way.

Kim took one look at Hannah and decided she'd said way more than enough. "Uh . . . I gotta go," she said, and trotted off down the hallway before Hannah could react.

Morgan swallowed hard as the horrible truth began to sink in. "Are you using Coleman so you can get better grades?" she whispered, stunned and disgusted.

"Hey," Hannah said, shrugging it off, "he's not complaining. My grades are up, and everybody's happy, right? See you later." She left Morgan standing there, speechless, and walked off, waving to Coleman, who had just appeared at the end of the hallway. Seeing Hannah, he beamed and waved back at her.

Morgan couldn't believe it! Hannah had

just admitted that she was only going out with Coleman because he was smart! And Coleman didn't have a clue! Morgan knew she couldn't let 'Slaw be played like this. She just couldn't.

"'Slaw!" she called to him. "Wait!"

Coleman turned and saw Morgan. But before he could respond, Hannah put her arm around him, and with a withering look at Morgan, said, "Let's get out of here. You don't want to hang out with her."

With that, Hannah led him away, leaving Morgan standing there—alone and powerless to help her friend.

CHAPTER SEVEN

DAMAGE CONTROL

That afternoon, the family brought Mr. Lighter home from the hospital. His right arm was in a cast up to the shoulder and a metal strut propped up the whole arm so that it stuck straight out at shoulder height.

Elliott brought up the rear—behind Mr. Lighter, Mrs. Lighter, Nick, and Nick's older sister, Hilary. Elliott had been sitting on the Lighters' front steps for hours, waiting for the family to get home so he could tell Mr. Lighter he was sorry.

Elliott knew it was all his fault. He never should have let Mr. Lighter get on that board!

"What were you thinking, getting on a skateboard?" Mrs. Lighter scolded, as she helped her husband maneuver through the front door. It was no easy job, either. Mr. Lighter had a three-foot wingspan with his arm stuck out like that. The cast kept banging into the side of the doorway, and Mr. Lighter yelped "Ow!" every time.

"I mean, really!" Mrs. Lighter said as she continued her good-natured lecture. "At your age?"

"So I had a little accident," Mr. Lighter said defensively.

Nick helped his dad through the doorway and inside the house. Elliott followed the others into the hallway, and closed the door behind him.

"Poor Daddy!" Hilary exclaimed, shaking her head in dismay. "What did those stooges do to you?"

"It was just one stooge," Elliott answered her. "Me."

"Elliott!" Mr. Lighter swung around to greet him. As he did, his outstretched cast slammed into a potted plant, knocking it down. Nick leaped for it, catching the pot just before it hit the floor.

Mr. Lighter didn't notice. Unable to look to his right without swinging around, he did so now, to see what all the yelling was about—and knocked over a glass vase full of flowers. This time, no one could make the save.

They all stared at the shattered glass littering the floor—all of them except Mr.

Lighter, who could not look down because of the brace around his upper torso.

"Maybe you should sit down," Mrs. Lighter suggested gently.

"Good idea," Mr. Lighter meekly agreed. He sidestepped his way into the den, turned to face forward again, and sent a table lamp toppling over. The lightbulb went out with a pop. Finally, Mr. Lighter sank onto the sofa, a pained expression on his face.

"Now, you stay right there," Mrs. Lighter told him, heading for the kitchen, "and we'll bring you anything you need."

"Dad, you okay?" Nick asked, propping his father up with a pillow.

Elliott came up behind them. "Mr. Lighter?" he said. "You gave it up for freedom. Way to go!" He clapped him hard on the right shoulder.

"Yeow!" Mr. Lighter shrieked, grimacing in pain.

"Elliott!" Hilary scolded him.

Elliott backed away, wincing in shame. He had screwed up again!

"Honey? Are you okay?" Mrs. Lighter gasped as she came running back in.

"I'm . . . I'm okay . . . I'm okay," Mr. Lighter told her, with a tight little smile. "I'm fine. Just fine."

Elliott stepped back farther into the shadows, feeling guiltier than ever.

The MNFC had never spent a more dismal Monday night, Nick thought, sighing sadly as he stood at the front door, waving good-bye to 'Slaw and Hannah. Mr. Lighter had occupied one whole couch, and Coleman and Hannah somehow wound up on the other one. Nick, Elliott, and Morgan had all spent the whole time on the floor.

Morgan had barely said a word all night, and neither had Elliott. Hilary and Mrs. Lighter kept popping in and out of the den, asking if Mr. Lighter wanted anything—and never asking any of *them*. They'd stand there, right in front of the TV, blocking the view. And worst of all, the game hadn't even been close! Yes, all in all, a pretty miserable night, Nick reflected.

As Nick closed the front door, he had a sinking feeling that there would be one last negative to round out the evening. Just before the game ended, Morgan had leaned over and whispered to Nick and Elliott that she had to talk to them both— and from the look on her face, it wasn't going to be good news.

Nick went back into the den. Morgan and Elliott were already deep in conversation, and they both looked worried.

Morgan turned to Nick, and got right to the point. "Hannah's using 'Slaw," she told him. "She's on scholastic probation, and she told me she's using him to do all her work for her."

Nick shook his head in disbelief. "She actually said it?" he asked. "Out loud?"

"Yes!" Morgan insisted. "She's only using Coleman to get better grades. Once she's got what she wants, she'll probably dump him—and that would break his heart."

Elliott shook his head sadly. "Relationships are so complicated these days," he said with a heavy sigh.

"We have to tell him," Morgan insisted.

"How?" Nick asked.

"He's not going to want to hear it," Elliott said, furrowing his brow. "So . . . who's going to do it?" he asked, looking at Morgan, then at Nick, who both looked right back at him. "What?" he asked. "Hey, I don't want to tell him. He's bigger than me!"

Morgan and Elliott looked at Nick. With both their eyes on him, Nick suddenly felt afraid—not that Coleman would hurt him, but that he would hurt Coleman's feelings.

Morgan's jaw tightened, sensing Nick's reluctance. "Okay," she said, dropping her shoulders in surrender. "I'll do it. . . ."

"Uh, no offense, Morgan," said Elliott, getting up and going over to her. "But he's really not going to want it to come from a girl."

"Yeah," agreed Nick with a sigh.

Someone had to tell Coleman, and Nick guessed he was as good a man as any to do it. It would hurt 'Slaw, sure—but not as bad as Hannah dumping him once she was off scholastic probation.

"This isn't the kind of thing you want to hear in front of a group, either," Nick continued. "I'll do it." He put his arms around Elliott's and Morgan's shoulders, drawing them into a sort of huddle. "He and I have been best buds since the eighties," he said. "If 'Slaw can't hear it from me, he can't hear it from anybody."

Nick let the whole next day go by . . . and the next day, and the next . . . and still, he couldn't manage to find the right time to talk to Coleman. Meanwhile, he did his best to avoid Morgan and Elliott, so he wouldn't have to explain his delay.

Finally, on Thursday afternoon, after the last bell at school, Nick caught up with Coleman in the front lobby of the school. 'Slaw was standing there, watching the other kids pass by him on their way out of the building. He had a peaceful smile on his face.

"Good," Nick said to himself. "He's in a good mood. It's now or never." Stepping forward, he called out, "Hey, 'Slaw!"

Coleman waved to him, and Nick hustled over to his side. "'Slaw," he said, clapping him on the back, "we need to talk."

"Make it fast," Coleman told him, as a lovestruck smile spread over his face. "I'm meeting an angel dropped from heaven."

Nick couldn't believe it! This was the best news in the world. He wondered who this new "angel" could be. . . .

"Really?" he said. "So you broke up

with Hannah? Aw, man, this is great!"

He was about to tell Coleman how relieved he was that there was a new girl in Coleman's life, but 'Slaw backed away from him, a horrified look on his face. "No!" 'Slaw said, putting a hand up. "I meant I'm meeting *Hannah*."

"Oh!" Nick said, feeling himself blush with embarrassment. Talk about putting your foot in it! he said to himself disgustedly. "Exactly. Right," he muttered, fudging to cover his embarrassment.

Still, now that he'd opened his mouth, he couldn't hold back. Nick figured he might as well get the whole truth out, right here and right now. "Speaking of Hannah," he began.

Coleman cut him off. "What is wrong with you, man?" he asked, raising his voice in frustration.

"I have to tell you something," Nick insisted. "And you're not going to like it. And I'm really sorry."

"Nick. What?"

There. He had 'Slaw's attention now. He was looking at Nick, his brow furrowed anxiously.

"Hannah's no good for you, man," Nick told him flatly.

Coleman's expression hardened instantly.

"I'm serious," Nick pressed on. "She's only hanging out with you because you'll do her homework."

The pain in Coleman's eyes was plain as day. "But I *like* that she's hanging out with me," he told Nick, speaking as if to a little child who couldn't understand such things. "And you . . . you're supposed to be my friend. You should like it, too."

"Oh, 'Slaw . . ." Nick sighed, shaking his head sadly.

"She likes me for my mind. So?" Coleman challenged him.

"You think I wanted to tell you this?" Nick said.

Coleman wavered for a split second. Then they heard Hannah's voice, cooing "Cole-man!" from the far end of the hall.

'Slaw turned to go. Nick called after him, "She's on scholastic probation!"

Coleman turned back, and gave Nick a long, dark look. "You don't know what you're talking about," he whispered, and turned away again.

Again, Nick called out, louder this time. "And she's going to dump you once she has the grades—"

Coleman wheeled around, his eyes fierce with anger. "That's a lie!" he said, pointing an accusing finger at Nick.

"I'm not finished—" Nick said.

"I am." Coleman stopped him.

"'Slaw, you have to listen to me!" Nick pleaded.

"I don't *have* to do anything!" 'Slaw walked right up to Nick, until their faces were nearly touching. "Now get outta my face," he warned. Then he turned and walked away.

This time, Nick didn't try to stop him. He watched his friend walk off with Hannah, wondering if Coleman was walking out of his life—out of all their lives— forever.

Could this really be it? Nick wondered. Could this mean the end of the Monday Night Football Club?

CHAPTER EIGHT

A TOUCH OF MAGIC

Morgan was waiting outside the school for Nick. "How'd he take it?" Morgan asked, already wincing as if in pain. She must have seen him talking to 'Slaw, Nick figured—or maybe she'd guessed by the look on his face. In either case, it must have been obvious that things hadn't gone well.

"It was horrible," Nick moaned. "I don't know if he's ever going to talk to me again."

"We can't let him off that easy," Morgan said, determined to help Coleman. "We have to give it one more try."

"How?" Nick asked, feeling defeated. "She's always around."

"And he's so lost," Morgan added.

"And I'm so useless. . . ." Nick leaned back against a tree, closed his eyes, and slid slowly to the ground. "And as the saying goes, love is blind," he added.

"Yeah," Morgan said, gesturing across the front lawn of the school toward something that had caught her eye. "But is love stupid?"

Nick turned to see what she was staring at. There were Coleman and Hannah, sitting on the grass together. A biology book was open between them, and Hannah was whispering "sweet nothings" into Coleman's ear.

"If I could just get him away from her long enough to make him listen to—" Nick stopped in mid-sentence. He stared at the binder Morgan was carrying in her arms: the one with the picture of Tony Hawk on the cover. Suddenly, a lightbulb went off in his head.

"I've got an idea!" he said excitedly, jumping up. "Keep track of 'Slaw," he told Morgan as he ran off. "I'll be right back!"

"Wait!" Morgan called after him. "What are you going to do?"

Nick smiled over his shoulder and yelled, "I'm going take him to a place where Hannah can't get near him."

"Oh, brother," said Morgan with a sigh. It was all too easy for her to guess what Nick was up to. He was running home to get the jersey. Then he was going to use it to ambush Coleman—to jump the two of them to another place and into other bodies—so that they could finally talk about this Hannah situation.

Only recently had the MNFC discovered this part of the jersey's mechanics. At first, it had seemed that only Nick and Morgan could "jump" with the jersey. But then they discovered that if Nick or Morgan was touching another person while they had the jersey on, and if the timing was right, the jersey jumped both people.

But this was the first time that Nick was going to try to channel the jersey's powers for his own motives, Morgan thought as she kept her eyes glued on Coleman and Hannah. She sure hoped Nick's plan wouldn't backfire. 'Slaw was mad enough at him as it was.

• • •

As Nick blew into his house via the kitchen door, he nearly ran into his father, who was walking down the hall from the kitchen to the den. He was wearing his bathrobe, unfastened, and his arm in its cast stuck out as far as ever, knocking paintings crooked on the wall as he went.

Hilary trailed behind him, a glass of iced tea in her hand. "I've got your drink, Daddy. I'm right behind you."

Hearing this, Mr. Lighter turned around suddenly. Hilary had to duck to avoid the cast slamming right into her head. "Hil?" Mr. Lighter called, unable to see her crouching down at his feet. "Where'd you go?"

Just as she was getting up, he turned back the other way, and she had to duck once again—another near miss. Quickly, she handed him the glass, before he could hit anything else.

"Thanks, honey," he said, flashing her a grateful smile.

Nick couldn't stand there one second longer, waiting for them to clear out of the hallway. He had incredibly important things to do. He blew past them down the hall, doing his best broken-field running to get around Hilary and his father.

His dad spun around like a revolving door as Nick went by. Hilary ducked again. Her red hair flew every which way as the hard cast missed her head by a fraction of an inch.

"Sorry!" Nick called out, running into the den and over to the trophy case where he kept the magic jersey.

"Would you look at him!" Hilary complained to their father. "You're in pain and he doesn't even care!"

Their dad turned to look, and once again, Hilary ducked. She was getting good at this.

"No, no, no. I'm just fine," Mr. Lighter assured Hilary.

Nick rocketed back out of the den, down the hall, and right out the front door, accidentally pushing his dad's cast aside as he flew by. His dad spun around. Hilary ducked. "Missed me again!" she said with a giggle.

But this time, Hilary popped back up too soon. Unbeknownst to her, her dad was still spinning around. On his next rotation, the cast hit Hilary square on the head, and Hilary hit the floor. She was out cold.

"Hil'?" Mr. Lighter called. "Hil'? Hey, where'd everybody go?"

• • •

Coleman and Hannah were about to leave the school grounds when Nick finally got back there with the jersey. He found Morgan hiding behind a big tree.

"Good, you're finally back!" she said in a hushed tone. "Not a moment too soon, either. They're on the move. Okay, you take him, and I'll take her."

"I'm taking him, all right," Nick said, following her as they picked up their pace, getting closer and closer to Coleman and Hannah.

"Hey, Hannah!" Morgan called out as they came up behind the couple. "Hey, come here," she said, throwing an arm around the surprised Hannah's shoulders and drawing her off to one side and away from the guys. "How's it going?"

"What do *you* want?" Hannah asked, taken aback.

"Nothing," Morgan said airily. "Just shooting the breeze."

"So . . . shoot."

Morgan fumbled for something, anything to say—but all the while, she was drawing Hannah farther away from Coleman.

At the same time, Nick blocked Coleman's path, so he couldn't follow Hannah. "'Slaw!" he said, putting a hand on Coleman's shoulder. "We've gotta talk!"

Coleman grabbed Nick's wrist and removed it from his shoulder, then lightly shoved Nick in the chest. "What are you doing?" he demanded. "I suppose you didn't hear me clearly earlier. I'm not talking to you!"

"Just, uh, listen, 'Slaw . . . can you give me five minutes?" Nick put a hand out to restrain Coleman, but once again, Coleman knocked it aside. "Three minutes!" Nick continued, compromising. "Three minutes, that's all! All right?"

He pointed Coleman over to an area behind a tree, where Hannah couldn't see them. "Look, this is kind of private," he explained. "Can you just come over here for a minute?"

"Yeah, all right," Coleman grumbled, trudging on ahead of Nick. "You have eighteen seconds. Now what is it?"

He turned around, only to find that Nick had slipped the jersey on over his shirt while Coleman's back was turned! "Oh, no—get that thing away from me!" 'Slaw exclaimed, backing away.

Nick came toward him, and Coleman tried to break around him, to get back to where Hannah and Morgan were standing. "Don't come near me with that!" he warned Nick.

Nick paid no attention, of course. He did his best to corner Coleman, and wrap his arms around him. If he could do that much, Nick knew that the jersey would do the rest.

But somehow 'Slaw managed to get past him. Now Nick was chasing him as he ran toward Morgan and Hannah.

Morgan turned and saw what was happening. Stepping in between Hannah and Coleman so they couldn't see each other, she held up her books in front of her. 'Slaw ran right smack into them, allowing Nick to catch up.

He grabbed a hold of Coleman, and instantly he felt the jersey beginning to work its magic. The last thing Nick saw before they jumped was the picture of Tony Hawk on Morgan's binder.

CHAPTER NINE

DOUBLE SWITCH

Hannah looked around, bewildered. "I turn away for one second, and they're both gone! Poof—just like that. It's weird!" She looked hard at Morgan. "Where is Coleman?" she asked, her eyes narrowing with suspicion.

"I don't know," Morgan said, shrugging. "He just sort of got . . . pulled away." She flashed Hannah an innocent smile.

Well, it was the truth, Morgan thought. She didn't know where they'd gone—nobody did, except Nick and 'Slaw themselves.

One thing was for sure, though— Coleman was not with Hannah. And right now, that was all that mattered.

Nick could hear the now familiar roar of the crowd. Every time he jumped, it was like this. He was always some sports star or another, smack dab in the middle of the pro action. This time, he had a distinct feeling about which star he would turn out to be. . . .

He could feel himself in motion, rolling up a ramp at warp speed. Nick became vaguely aware that he was in a dark, noisy arena, filled with smoke for effect. Spotlights crisscrossed in the darkness, then trained on him as he did his skate-boarding routine.

He felt his body twisting acrobatically in a way it never had before. He did an airborne somersault, and landed perfectly on the down ramp. The crowd went wild, and Nick raised his arms above his head to acknowledge them. He rolled to the lip of the ramp and dismounted, taking a deep bow and holding his skateboard aloft.

"Ladies and gentlemen, the one and only Tony Hawk!" came the announcer's voice over the loudspeaker.

"I knew it!" Nick said under his breath. He had looked at that picture on Morgan's binder, and that's who he had jumped into. But what about 'Slaw? wondered Nick. Where was he? Had Nick succeeded in bringing him here?

"Nick!"

It had to be Coleman's voice calling him. Who else would know that it was really Nick inside Tony Hawk's body? Now that Nick had a chance to look around the arena, he could see that there were actually three ramps, side by side, each with different features, slopes, and obstacles. On the far lip of one of the other ramps, Nick saw Dave Mirra, "The Miracle Man"—one of the world's greatest trick bikers, and one of Coleman's big heroes.

"Nick!" Dave Mirra was shouting. "Wherever you are, you're gonna be very sorry!" It was 'Slaw; it had to be.

"Coleman!" Nick shouted. "Over here!"

Dave Mirra looked over at Nick with daggers in his eyes.

The announcer's voice rang out again. "Hawk and Mirra, together in action! Not a bad way to spend the afternoon!"

The crowd cheered, the noise echoing off the walls of the arena. It was so loud, Nick could actually feel the building shaking. He could see that the crowd was not only filling all the available seating; there were also people standing on the arena floor, kept away from the ramps by a ten-foot-high chain-link fence.

"Come on, Dave, it's your turn!" the announcer's voice echoed.

Frowning, Coleman straddled his bike and took off down the ramp of the half-pipe, doing incredible aerials, twists, and wheelies as the crowd went wild.

"Well," Nick told himself as he watched, "at least 'Slaw gets to have a taste of what it's like to be a professional trick-biker. I'll have to remind him of that later." But in the back of his mind, Nick was sure that unless he got through to Coleman right here and now, they wouldn't be spending much time together later. His friend would soon be his *ex*-friend.

"I can't believe you jumped me here!" Coleman yelled as he went airborne not far from where Nick was standing. Then he launched into an incredible, gravity-defying jump, hanging in midair for what seemed like forever and spinning his front wheel around in rapid circles, before coming back down and pulling his bike to a halt at the bottom of the ramp.

Wild applause erupted as Nick pushed off and rolled down to join him. "'Slaw, we've gotta talk!" he pleaded.

"No way!" Coleman shot back. "I'm not talking to you! I finally like a girl who likes me back, and you're not going to mess that up!"

"But she's just using you for her

homework!" Nick insisted.

Just then, a boy about Nick and Coleman's age burst through the open gate of the chain-link fence, carrying his board under one arm and a permanent marker in the other hand.

"Whoa! No autographs—please!" the announcer called, but the boy kept right on running until he was standing next to Nick. He held out the board and the marker to Nick, asking for an autograph.

Without thinking, Nick quickly scribbled his name on the board and turned back to Coleman.

"Hey!" the kid said, frowning at the signature. "Who's 'Nick Lighter'?"

"Nick, you're supposed to be Tony Hawk," Coleman reminded him. The kid gave both of them a funny look.

"Oops!" Nick said. "Here, give me that

back." He took the board and marker, and wrote "Tony Hawk" on the other end of the board. This time, the kid gave him a big smile and exited through the gate, leaving Nick and Coleman alone again.

"You'd better get me out of here now, Nick!" 'Slaw demanded.

"No! Not until you listen!"

"Forget it!"

"Dave Mirra," called the announcer over the loudspeaker, "you're still up, man. Head over to the main ramp."

"If you'll excuse me," Coleman said, giving Nick a sour look, "I've got an exhibition to perform."

Back at the high school, Hannah was searching for Coleman, peeking behind trees and parked cars, while Morgan tried hard to get rid of her.

"Look, Coleman obviously had other plans," Morgan told her. "So . . . let's all just go home," she suggested.

Hannah wheeled around and pointed a finger in Morgan's face. "Coleman knows I have a biology paper due tomorrow. I'm not going anywhere."

"What's the matter?" Morgan asked, with a sly smile. "Can't do it without The 'Slaw?"

Hannah opened her mouth as if to fire back a defense—but then, her shoulders slumped, and she turned away from Morgan without a word.

After all, what could she say? Morgan was right, and they both knew it.

Nick followed Coleman up the ramp, his skateboard under one arm. "I'm telling you, man: she's using you!" he called after his friend. 'Slaw didn't turn around, so Nick brought out his ace in the hole. "Morgan heard it from the source!" he said.

Coleman turned to face him, disbelief written all over his face. "Hannah *said* that?" he asked.

"Yes, she did!"

"Yeah, right." Coleman snorted derisively.

"Look," Nick said, putting a hand on Coleman's shoulder. "I'm not saying she doesn't like you. Who wouldn't like you?"

Coleman sighed. "Um, let's see— Danielle, Nicole, Tara, Michelle—need I go on?"

"I'm not trying to wreck your relationship, 'Slaw. You've gotta believe me."

"Well, it sure seems that way!" Coleman said, staring Nick down with a cold look that froze Nick to the spot.

"Dave Mirra!" the announcer's voice rang out with a tone of mock scolding. "The lovely ladies and gentlemen aren't paying their money to watch your tea party. Let's see some action!"

Coleman gave Nick one last look, and pedaled off, rocketing down the ramp. He flew into the air on the upside, spinning his front wheel around several times in midair before coming back down to earth.

Nick set his jaw and pushed off after Coleman. This was his last chance to save 'Slaw. He had to keep trying!

"Wow!" the announcer shouted. "Guys, this is insane! Dave Mirra, the Miracle Man, and the legendary Tony Hawk, together in action! Revolutionaries in each of their sports—on the ramps at the same time! Ladies and gentlemen, this is a

totally spontaneous demonstration of skill, not listed on your program! It's just an amazing demo by two real superstars!"

Nick and Coleman whizzed by each other again and again, each of them doing stunts they could never have done as themselves. The crowd was at fever pitch, but over the noise Nick could still make out 'Slaw's voice calling to him as they passed at mid-ramp. "Nick! You're wrong!" he shouted. "I'll prove it!"

When Coleman came his way again, Nick noticed the determined look on his face. "'Slaw!" he yelled.

But Coleman had only one thought on his mind. "Take me back—now!" he demanded.

Nick rode to the top of the ramp and skated back down. There was no mistaking the tone in 'Slaw's voice. Nick knew there was no point in dragging this out any longer. But on the next pass, before Nick could concede, Coleman took matters into his own hands. He reached out and grabbed Nick's shirt, knowing it was the trigger that would send Nick and himself back to their real lives.

There was a whooshing sound as Coleman's hand made contact, then a flash of blue light, and the next thing Nick knew, he and 'Slaw were floating through space. The roar of the arena crowd was now just a fading echo.

They were on their way back—to face the truth.

CHAPTER TEN

MOMENT OF TRUTH

Morgan had not given up. She was still trying to get Hannah out of there before Coleman and Nick jumped back. They had been gone a good ten minutes, and from past experience, Morgan knew they could be back any second.

Hannah was getting tired of waiting; Morgan could see that. She was pacing up and down by the spot where she'd last seen 'Slaw. Morgan could read the annoyance on Hannah's face, and it gave her satisfaction to think that she and Nick were at least doing all they could to save Coleman from this girl's evil motives.

"I give up," Hannah finally said, throwing up her hands. "Tell Coleman I'll call him later."

"I'll do that for sure," Morgan replied, crossing her fingers as Hannah turned to go.

Morgan breathed a sigh of relief as she watched her go. "Good," she said to herself. "Another few seconds and she'll be out of sight."

Just then, though, she heard a soft whooshing sound behind her. Morgan turned to see a flash of blue light, and suddenly, Nick and 'Slaw were rolling on the ground in front of her!

Coleman got up like a shot, and looked

around him. "Hannah!" he cried out, spotting her retreating figure just before she turned around the corner of the school and disappeared from view. "Hannah! Wait! Here I am!"

"Dang!" Morgan said under her breath, as Coleman shot Morgan and Nick a furious look, then took off down the sidewalk after his lady love.

Nick got up and came over to Morgan's side, shaking his head sadly. They both watched as Hannah marched back in their direction, meeting 'Slaw halfway.

"Where did you go?" Morgan heard her say, an angry tone in her raised voice.

"Sorry," Coleman told her. "I got pulled away. I had to talk to a 'friend.'" He cast another hostile glance at Nick.

"Let's go already!" Hannah demanded, grabbing Coleman by the wrist and pulling him away. "I've got my biology assignment, plus a Spanish quiz!"

Morgan saw the hesitation in Coleman's face. For a second, he resisted Hannah's tug, and looked back at his friends, obviously feeling confused. Nick and Morgan both shook their heads and mouthed the word "no" to warn 'Slaw against going with Hannah.

Coleman hesitated for another instant, and then turned to Hannah. "Let's go study," he said, giving in. In a moment, both of them were gone, disappearing around the corner.

Morgan felt herself deflate, like the air going out of a tire. She could see that Nick was feeling the same way.

"I guess I blew it," he said, heaving a heavy sigh of defeat.

"You did the best you could, Nick,"

Morgan said, putting an arm around her cousin's shoulders. "You can't *make* him believe us."

"I can't believe he's really gone," Nick said softly, swallowing hard. "All these years . . . and everything changes. . . ." He let Morgan lead him away, leaning his head on her shoulder as they went.

This is a sad day for the MNFC, Morgan thought. And wait until Elliott finds out—he's going to hit the roof!

The next day was Friday—the day before Elliott would get his own skateboard back. But as hard as he tried, Elliott couldn't get excited about it. He felt horrible. He'd lost his best friend in the whole world. All day long, he'd moved through school like a zombie, barely able to pay attention in class. It had been sheer torture, and it wasn't about to get better any time soon.

He stared across the hallway to where Coleman stood by his open locker. 'Slaw didn't look any happier than Elliott felt—but that didn't mean they would ever be friends again.

It was the end of everything—of their friendship, of the MNFC. . . .

Morgan and Nick stood next to Elliott, watching Coleman as Elliott took his stuff out of his locker. But 'Slaw avoided their gaze.

"I called him all night," Nick said sadly, "but he didn't answer or return my calls."

"Should we talk to him?" Morgan asked.

"I don't know," Nick replied. "What if he won't talk to *us*? I mean, he knows we're here."

"Such a sad day for what was once the

MNFC," Elliott said with a sigh. "I feel so alone."

At that very moment, they heard Hannah's voice ring out from down the hall. "Coleman!" she shouted, rushing by the three of them while making a beeline for 'Slaw's locker. Elliott noticed that she was holding up a paper—and she definitely did *not* look pleased.

"I got a D on my biology report!" she shouted at Coleman. "And it's all your fault!"

Coleman grimaced, as if he sympathized. "Gosh, that's . . . that's bad," he said. "Guess you can't count on me to do all your homework, huh?" He looked deeply into her eyes, as if he could see right through her.

Hannah held his gaze for a long, agonizing moment, as his words sank in. She opened her mouth to say something, but she couldn't seem to find the words. Her mouth flapped open and shut, open and shut, but nothing came out except an incoherent little squeak of frustration. Then she slowly lowered her gaze to the floor, turned, and retreated down the hallway. Coleman watched her go with a look of pain and grief on his face.

Elliott blinked rapidly, not believing what he'd just seen. Looking at Morgan and Nick, he saw that they were just as flabbergasted. 'Slaw had done it! He'd kissed off Hard-hearted Hannah—sent her packing, told her *adiós*!

Well, that was great, Elliott reasoned. But it didn't mean 'Slaw was ever going to be friends with any of *them* again—not after the way they'd driven him and his first love apart.

Elliott stood rooted to the spot, waiting. He could almost feel Nick and Morgan holding their breath, just as he was.

Coleman shut his locker, still looking lost and sad. He trudged slowly toward them, slinging his yellow book bag over his shoulder, his eyes on the ground.

But then, as he approached them, 'Slaw's expression slowly began to change. Little by little, the dark cloud lifted, and a smile began to break out on his face. By the time he'd reached them, 'Slaw was beaming—a real Coleman smile to light up the whole school.

"Had you guys goin', didn't I?" he said, offering his hand.

Elliott grabbed it, giving 'Slaw the old MNFC handshake. There was cheering all around, and the happy hugs of reunited friends.

"Glad to have you back, man!" Nick said.

Coleman turned to Nick. "Back at you, man," he said, nodding. "Good thing you thought of the jersey." His eyes twinkled. "That was some riding we did, huh?"

Coleman high-fived Nick again, then came over to Elliott. "I've missed you, man."

"Same here."

'Slaw threw an arm around Elliott's shoulder. Morgan did the same to Nick. Soon they were walking down the hallway together, four friends headed for the exit, an unbeatable, unbreakable team once again.

CHAPTER ELEVEN

FREE AT LAST!

The next morning, Elliott's parents drove him down to the police station to get his board back. He had to stand there, listening to one more lecture on safety, common courtesy, citizenship, and reading the signs.

Elliott took it like a man. He could have waited even longer if he had to. Coleman was his buddy again, and the MNFC was alive and kicking. His half-pipe was waiting for him, and a minute or two more or less wasn't going to kill him.

When his mom dropped him off at the parking lot of the sporting-goods store, everyone was already there waiting for him: Nick, Morgan, Coleman, Mr. Lighter—still in his cast—and even Hilary. Elliott got out and ran over to them, holding his board aloft. "Free at last!" he cried.

He climbed up onto the lip of the half-pipe and looked down at the rest of them. "Hey, have you guys tried it out yet?" he asked. Morgan and Nick had their boards, and Coleman was on his bike.

"No, man," Nick told him. "It's your half-pipe. You've got to be the first."

"I owe it all to you, Mr. Lighter—I mean, Larry," Elliott said, saluting him.

"All for a good cause, huh?" Larry said

cheerfully, smiling in spite of his broken arm.

"Remind me to sign that cast of yours," Elliott said, fastening the chinstrap of his helmet.

"Hey, you know, when I get out of this cast, and get some elbow pads, I'll bet I could bust a few good moves," Mr. Lighter said, eyeing the half-pipe with longing.

"Daddy?" Hilary said, ducking as her father turned to face her.

"Yes, sweetheart?"

"No," answered Hilary flatly, squelching her father's skateboarding dreams.

Larry smiled weakly, sighed, and shrugged. "Well, maybe not," he said, backing down.

"Okay, here goes," Elliott said, launching himself down the ramp. He shrieked with joy as he hurtled into the air above the opposite lip. Spinning around, he came back down goofy-style, and when he reached the other side, did a step-walk on the lip before plunging down yet again.

Elliott didn't stop until he was totally worn out. It was the best routine he'd ever done! "I love this thing!" he cried as he stepped off and took a bow for the others.

They whooped and hollered and clapped their hands. "This rocks so much!" Morgan said, climbing up to take her turn.

Elliott hopped down off the half-pipe and went over to Nick. "That was awesome, Elliott," Nick said, high-fiving him.

"Hey, thanks!" he told Nick. "And now that I have my own half-pipe, I'll be as good as Tony Hawk in no time!"

"Uh, Ell?" Nick was looking at him with one raised eyebrow, shaking his head. "Man, you're good, but I *was* Tony Hawk, remember? And *nobody's* that good."

"Well, maybe not *that* good," Elliott conceded. "But the best boarder this town has ever seen!"

"For sure!" Nick said, and they pounded fists.

Elliott felt a quick pang of envy over the fact that Nick had gotten to jump as Tony Hawk; the "Hawkster" was *his* idol, after all, not Nick's. But then again, how upset could he be? It was a beautiful day, he had his board again, his half-pipe was a thing of beauty—and best of all, 'Slaw was back.

Coleman spoke up now, as Morgan got off the half-pipe. "I'd better go next," he said. "Then I've got to split. I've got a ton of homework to do."

Nick, Morgan, and Elliott all exchanged nervous glances. "It's *your* homework, isn't it?" Nick asked tentatively.

A sly grin came over Coleman's face, and they all relaxed, smiling back. "I've fallen behind a little bit the past few weeks," 'Slaw admitted. "Been too busy doing other people's work." He pulled his bike onto the half-pipe. "Here," he said, "lemme show you all a little something I picked up from Dave Mirra."

He pedaled his bike up the side of the ramp. But he didn't have enough speed going into his climb, and just as he got to the top of the ramp, the bike tumbled back over him, sending Coleman sprawling and rolling down into the middle of the half-pipe. Clearly, the mind was willing, but the body was no longer endowed with

Dave Mirra's super ability.

Nick chuckled, applauding. "'Slaw, that's amazing!"

"Yeah!" Morgan agreed, helping Coleman to his feet. "I've never seen Dave Mirra do *anything* like that!"

They all laughed, clapping Coleman on the back. Elliott held his board up between them, and they all grabbed it—friends again, now and forever.

CHAPTER TWO

STRIKE ONE, YOU'RE OUT!

"You can't cut somebody after one at-bat!" Elliott blurted. "That's some kind of . . . discrimination!"

"Blah, blah, blah," the coach mocked him, smiling a crooked smile. "Tell it to your lawyer."

Elliott headed for the dugout, simmering with frustration.

The coach turned away, then took up a bat and a ball. "Hey, girlie!" he called out to Morgan. "All right, it's your turn. Look alive!"

Elliott turned and watched as the coach hit a sharp grounder to Morgan. She fielded it cleanly, and tossed a strike to first base.

Great, Elliott thought. She's gonna make the team, and I'm not. How totally humiliating!

Sitting in the dugout with him were the other kids who had already been cut. Elliott squirmed uncomfortably. These kids weren't athletes—not like *he* was! Okay, so baseball wasn't his best sport, but he didn't belong with these scrubs! Most of them were even shorter than he was!

"Why me?" he asked out loud. "Always me! Protein shakes, vitamins. And for what? It's a conspiracy against the little guy, I tell you!"

Elliott felt a sudden knot of tension forming in his stomach. "Hey," he asked the kid sitting next to him, "how do you know if you're getting an ulcer?"

The kid just stared back at him, which only made Elliott more furious. *My baseball career is over before it's even begun, and this kid is looking at me like I'm crazy!* Elliott figured he'd better do something to release his frustration.

Elliott spied a bucket of baseballs on the ground next to him and gave it a vicious kick. The bucket spilled over, and the balls rolled out, bumping a stack of bats nearby. The bats began to topple over like a bunch of dominoes. Finally, the last bat went over. It hit the lever of an idle baseball pitching cannon.

Suddenly, the cannon went into action. It wound up and fired a curveball right through the dugout and onto the field, where it hit Coach Bender with a thud. Right between the eyes!

The coach dropped to the ground. A huge gasp of horror went up from all the assembled kids.

"Uh-oh," said Elliott.

Now he'd done it!

THE JERSEY

When the members of the MNFC try out for the school's baseball team, The Jersey "jumps" Morgan into the ring with boxer Laila Ali. That's when Morgan learns it's not easy to be a woman in a man's sport.

Does Morgan have what it takes?

FIND OUT IN THE JERSEY #7:

FIGHT FOR YOUR RIGHT

AVAILABLE IN BOOKSTORES MAY 2001

It'll knock you out!